Literacy Consultants
DAVID BOOTH • KATHLEEN GOULD LUNDY

Social Studies Consultant
PETER PAPPAS

A Harcourt Achieve Imprint

10801 N. Mopac Expressway
Building # 3
Austin, TX 78759
1.800.531.5015

Steck-Vaughn is a trademark of Harcourt Achieve Inc. registered in the United
States of America and/or other jurisdictions. All inquiries should be mailed to:
Paralegal Department, 6277 Sea Harbor Drive, Orlando, FL 32887.

Ru'bicon © 2007 Rubicon Publishing Inc.
www. rubiconpublishing.com

Project Editor: Kim Koh
Editor: Vicki Low
Art Director: Jen Harvey
Project Designer: Jan-John Rivera

7 8 9 10 11   5 4 3 2 1

Trapped in Gallipoli
ISBN 13: 978-1-4190-3211-0
ISBN 10:   1-4190-3211-9

Printed in Singapore

PHOTO CREDITS: istockphoto: 2-5, 13, 21, 29, 37, 45-47; The Granger Collection,
New York: 4, 29; Bettmann/Corbis: 13, 21; Hulton-Deutsch Collection: 37

TRAPPED IN GALLIPOLI

Written by
BARBARA WINTER

Illustrated by
SCOTT PAGE

DUYAL

REAL PEOPLE IN HISTORY

MUSTAFA KEMAL

MUSTAFA KEMAL (1881–1938): The Turkish commander at Gallipoli.

WILLIAM BIRDWOOD (1865–1951): The Australian general in charge of the ANZAC troops.

WILLIAM BIRDWOOD

FICTIONAL CHARACTERS

DUYAL: The 10-year-old son of Mustafa Kemal's cousin.

JACK SWAN: An Australian soldier who becomes Duyal's friend during the campaign.

JACK SWAN

Contents

4   **Introduction**

6   **Chapter 1: Attack from the Sea**
13   **Time Out:** The Troops at Gallipoli

14   **Chapter 2: Battle for Gallipoli**
21   **Time Out:** Life at Gallipoli

22   **Chapter 3: Captured by Enemy Troops**
29   **Time Out:** The ANZACS

30   **Chapter 4: War Without End**
37   **Time Out:** Weapons Used

38   **Chapter 5: Victory at Last!**
45   **Time Out:** The Allies Withdraw

46   **Moving On: The Legacy of Gallipoli**

Troops at war

The First World War lasted from 1914 to 1918. It was fought between the Allies (Britain, France, Russia, and the United States) and the Central Powers (Germany, Austria-Hungary, Turkey, and Bulgaria). Countries that were part of the British Empire — Canada, Australia, and New Zealand — fought on the side of the Allies.

TIMELINE

1915: Jan. 13 »»	Feb. 19–25 »»	Mar. 22 »»	Apr. 25 »»	Apr. 28 »»
The British plan an attack through the Dardanelles channel.	British and French ships attack Turkish forts along the Dardanelles.	The British decide on an attack by both land and sea.	The British, French, and ANZAC troops land on the Gallipoli Peninsula.	The first of three battles takes place. Allies suffer heavy losses.

EUROPE

Gallipoli
Peninsula

Dardanelles

TURKEY

Gallipoli is the name of the peninsula (piece of land jutting into the sea) in western Turkey where fighting between the Allies and Turkish troops took place. The Gallipoli Peninsula was important because of its location. It overlooked the Dardanelles, a narrow channel between the Mediterranean and the Black Sea. Whoever won control of the Dardanelles would have power over Constantinople (now Istanbul), the capital of Turkey.

The Allies launched the Gallipoli campaign in April 1915. It was an important mission for the Allies. They thought they would win the war quickly if they could defeat the Turks at Gallipoli. But could they?

WHAT'S THE STORY?

This story is set in an actual time in history and depicts real people, but some of the characters and events are fictitious.

May 24 »	Aug. 10 »	Nov. 27–30 »	Dec. 19 »	1916: Jan. 9 »
Both sides declare a pause in the fighting in order to bury their dead.	A British attack fails.	Many die in a great blizzard at Gallipoli.	Allied troops pull out of Gallipoli.	The last Allied troops leave Gallipoli.

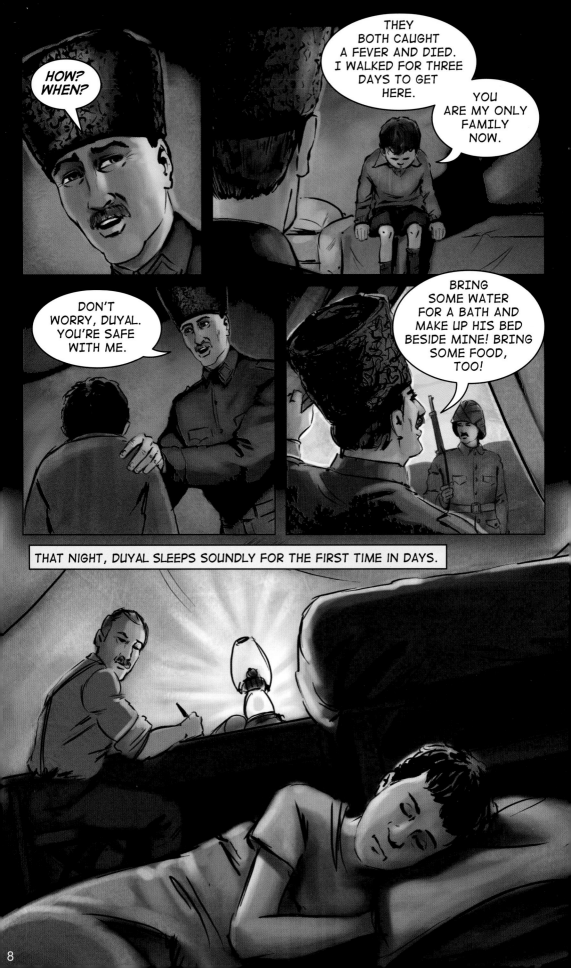

THE GENERALS SAY THREE DAYS AT MOST.
DO YOU REALLY BELIEVE THAT?
THE ALLIED TROOPS FROM AUSTRALIA AND NEW ZEALAND (THE ANZACS) LAND ON THE BEACH, BUT ...
THIS IS THE WRONG BEACH! IT'S TOO SMALL AND THE CLIFFS ARE TOO STEEP!
WHAT WENT WRONG?
I DON'T KNOW. THE CURRENT MAY HAVE BEEN TOO STRONG. SOMEONE HAS MADE A MISTAKE.
TOO LATE TO COMPLAIN, MATE! WE HAVE TO MAKE THE BEST OF THIS NOW.

Allied troops landing
on Gallipoli

THE TROOPS AT GALLIPOLI

Mustafa Kemal

THE TURKISH: The Turks fought on the side of the Central Powers against the Allies. Their commander was Mustafa Kemal.

THE BRITISH: Of the Allies, the British sent the most troops and battleships.

THE FRENCH: The French sent many troops and battleships to Gallipoli. At the time, many battles were being fought in France.

THE ANZACS: The ANZACS were soldiers from Australia and New Zealand. *ANZAC* stands for Australia and New Zealand Army Corps.

OTHERS: The Allied force also included soldiers from Ireland, Newfoundland, India, and Ceylon (now Sri Lanka). There was also a troop of Jewish volunteers.

A FEW WEEKS LATER. THE ALLIES HAVE ADVANCED ON THE PENINSULA, BUT THEY HAVE MET WITH FIERCE FIGHTING FROM THE TURKISH ARMY. BOTH SIDES HAVE DUG THEMSELVES INTO TRENCHES. FOOD IS SCARCE, AND MANY ARE DEAD OR INJURED.

IN KEMAL'S TENT ...

SUCH A WASTE OF MEN'S LIVES! WHY DON'T THEY GIVE UP? THEY KNOW WE WILL NEVER ALLOW THEM TO SUCCEED!

I'M AFRAID THIS MAY GO ON FOR A WHILE, COMMANDER KEMAL. THE LOSSES ARE VERY HEAVY ON BOTH SIDES.

STAND UP, SOLDIER!

SORRY, SIR!

WHO ARE YOU?

PRIVATE JACK SWAN OF THE SEVENTH BATTALION, SIR!

In the trenches

LIFE AT GALLIPOLI

The Gallipoli campaign lasted for eight months through the hot summer and freezing winter. On both sides, soldiers lived in trenches — long ditches dug into the ground — with little protection from the weather. When it rained, the ground turned to mud.

Allied soldiers ate bully (corned beef in cans) and biscuits, and drank a lot of tea. Turkish soldiers had soup, bread, olives, and a kind of crushed wheat called bulgur.

When soldiers weren't fighting, they wrote letters home and kept diaries. They also spent a lot of time getting rid of lice on their bodies and clothes. Just as many soldiers died from disease as from battle wounds.

DUYAL TRIES TO HELP THE WOUNDED TURKISH SOLDIERS.

I'M HERE TO HELP YOU! HERE'S SOME WATER.

O-O-O-H ...

A GRENADE COMES FLYING OUT OF THE ALLIED TRENCH!

OH NO!

27

AUSTRALIA

NEW ZEALAND

ANZAC troops

THE ANZACS

The ANZACs were excellent soldiers, but they were known to be less orderly and respectful of authority than British troops. Australia and New Zealand together sent many troops to Gallipoli.

The ANZACs used slang words and phrases to make fun of the poor conditions at Gallipoli. An "ANZAC button" was a nail used to hold up trousers when a button fell off. "ANZAC stew" was whatever hot food could be made from their supplies. If a soldier had diarrhea, he had the "Gallipoli gallop"! A good friend was a "cobber."

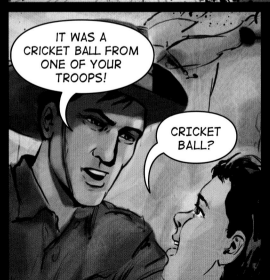

IN AUGUST, THERE IS A TERRIBLE BATTLE THAT LEAVES THOUSANDS OF SOLDIERS DEAD ON BOTH SIDES.

THE GENERALS AGREE TO STOP FIGHTING FOR A FEW DAYS. THEY WANT TO BURY THEIR DEAD SOLDIERS.

THE TURKISH AND ALLIED SOLDIERS MEET ON THE BATTLEFIELD DURING THIS PAUSE IN FIGHTING. DESPITE MONTHS OF WAR AGAINST ONE ANOTHER, THEY ARE FRIENDLY ...

IT SNOWS FOR MANY DAYS.

WEAPONS USED

Besides explosives, the main weapon used at Gallipoli was the howitzer — a short gun. When howitzer shells exploded, they scattered tiny steel balls and splinters. This scattered shot, called shrapnel, caused terrible injuries.

The British navy played a big part in the Gallipoli campaign. They sent the *HMS Ark Royal* — one of the first aircraft carriers with seaplanes on board. From these planes, soldiers found out where the Turkish guns were located. They also dropped explosives on enemy ships.

The Allied soldiers made do with what they had. They made bombs out of empty jam cans filled with stones and pieces of metal. Australian soldiers invented the periscope rifle, which they used to aim and shoot while staying safely in the trenches.

A damaged weapon on the Dardanelles beach

THE ALLIES REACH A DECISION. IN THE MIDDLE OF A COLD WINTER'S NIGHT, THEY PREPARE TO LEAVE.

FAREWELL, MATE. YOU'VE BEEN A GREAT COBBER TO ME. I'LL MISS YOU.

THE NEXT MORNING ...

WHAT? WHERE IS EVERYONE? WHERE DID THEY ALL GO?

40

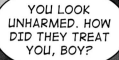

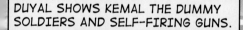

Dummy soldiers

THE ALLIES WITHDRAW

After eight months of fighting, the Allied High Command realized that they could not win at Gallipoli. In November 1915, the Allies decided to withdraw from the Gallipoli Peninsula.

In many ways, the withdrawal was the most successful part of the Allied campaign. The Allied soldiers left dummies of themselves and set guns to fire automatically so that the Turks would not suspect that they were leaving. They succeeded. The Turks did not find out about the withdrawal until after the Allies had left.

The troops started leaving in December. The wounded were removed first. Then the soldiers crept down from the hills and left in boats. The last of the Allied troops left in January 1916.

THE LEGACY OF

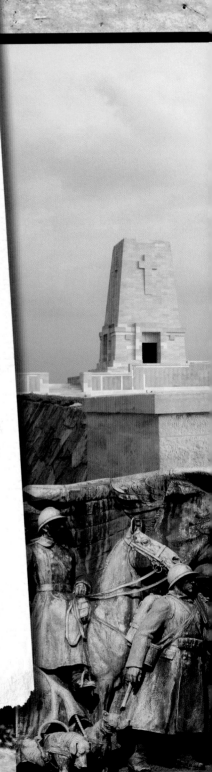

Mustafa Kemal was called the "Savior of Constantinople" for defending Gallipoli and the Dardanelles from the Allied attack of 1915. After the war, Kemal became the first president of the Turkish Republic in 1923. Kemal was called Ataturk, "Father of the Turks."

The Allies eventually won the First World War. But nobody knows exactly how many soldiers died at Gallipoli. It is estimated that the Turks lost about 87,000 men; the British about 22,000; and the French about 10,000. The ANZAC loss was about 8,000 for the Australians and nearly 3,000 for the New Zealanders.

A war memorial was set up at Gallipoli in 1934, with these words written by Kemal Ataturk:

Those heroes who shed their blood and lost their lives, you are now lying in the soil of a friendly country. Therefore, rest in peace. ... You, the mothers who sent your sons from faraway countries, wipe away your tears. Your sons are now lying in our bosom and are in peace. After having lost their lives on this land, they have become our sons as well.

GALLIPOLI

War memorial at Gallipoli

LONE PINE

April 25 — the day the Allies landed at Gallipoli — has become ANZAC Day in Australia and New Zealand. Like Veterans Day and Memorial Day, it is a day for remembering soldiers killed in battle.

INDEX

A
Allies, 4–5, 9, 13–14, 19, 24, 36, 38, 45–47
Ankara, 15
ANZACs, 4, 11, 13, 28–29, 33, 40, 46–47
Australia, 4, 11, 13, 26, 29, 47
Austria-Hungary, 4

B
Birdwood, General, 17–18
Black Sea, 5
Britain, 4
Bulgaria, 4

C
Canada, 4
Central Powers, 4, 13
Ceylon, 13
Constantinople, 5, 9, 46

D
Dardanelles, 4–5, 9, 46
Duyal, 7–9, 15–16, 19–20, 22–23, 26–28, 30, 33, 35, 40–43

F
First World War, 4, 46
France, 4, 13

G
Gallipoli, 4–6, 12–14, 21, 29, 37, 45–47
Germany, 4

I
India, 13
Ireland, 13
Istanbul, *see* Constantinople

K
Kemal, Mustafa, 6–7, 13–14, 27, 36, 43, 46

M
Mediterranean, 5
Melbourne, 18
Memorial Day, 47

N
New Zealand, 4, 11, 13, 29, 47
Newfoundland, 13

R
Russia, 4

S
Sea of Marmara, 9
Sri Lanka, *see* Ceylon
Swan, Jack, 10, 12, 17–18, 23, 26, 30, 35, 40

T
Trenches, 14, 21
Turkey, 4–6, 9

V
Veterans Day, 47

U
United States, 4